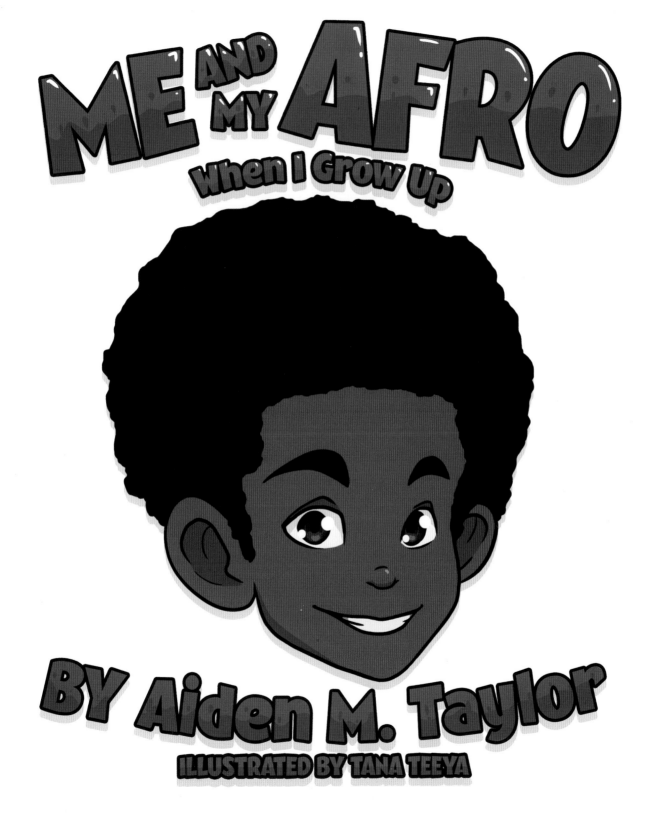

ME AND MY AFRO
When I Grow Up

BY Aiden M. Taylor
ILLUSTRATED BY TANA TEEYA

250 East 54th Street, Suite P2
New York, New York 10022

www.lightswitchlearning.com

Educators and Librarians, for a variety of teaching resources, visit www.lightswitchlearning.com.

Cover design and illustrations by Tana Teeya

ISBN: 978-1-7354085-2-1

Printed in China

This book belongs to : _____

Or maybe I will be a police officer and help people.

I can be a principal and make my school awesome.

9

Or a librarian and share amazing stories with everyone I know.

10

Or a dentist to keep people's teeth healthy.

12

How about a veterinarian to help our furry friends?

13

HOLLYWOOD

Ooh, I know...maybe I will be a famous movie star and be seen in movies everywhere!

14

Or a singer who performs in front of millions of people on stages all over the world.

15

I love sports, so maybe I can be a professional basketball player and shoot some hoops!

18

Or a baseball player who hits the ball really far.

19

Or a bus driver who gets people where they want to go.

22

I can be a chef, and people will enjoy my yummy food.

23

Or a scientist who invents new and exciting things.

24

I can be a pilot and soar high in the sky!

25

Or an astronaut who explores space.

Or a barber so I can make me and my Afro look great!

27

Hmmm......

30

Which one should I choose??

I am not sure what I want to be just yet, but I have lots of time to think about it.

Do YOU know what you want to be when you grow up?

34

About The Author

Aiden M. Taylor is an eleven-year-old writer, actor, and model. He has been viewed by millions in television commercials, featured in print advertisements, and seen on one of the largest billboards in Times Square. Aiden has been featured on *ABC Eyewitness News*, on *NBC Nightly News with Lester Holt: Kids Edition* and in *People Magazine* for his wildly successful debut as an author for his first release, *Me And My Afro*, which promotes self-love. With his new follow-up, *When I Grow Up*, Aiden has another important message for his young readers: You can be anything you want if you set your mind to it!

When Aiden is not writing uplifting books for children or working as an actor and model, he can be found pursuing his many interests and passions. He loves basketball, video games, poetry, math, and learning new things. He is a proud "Little Brother" in the Big Brothers Big Sisters of New York City program.